The Magic Shoebox Farm

To Sophie and Amelie with loads of love.

Toolboxes to follow… Ok? – I.W.

To Harvey – P.H.

First published in paperback in Great Britain
by HarperCollins Children's Books in 2007

ISBN-13: 978-0-00-783786-1
1 3 5 7 9 10 8 6 4 2

HarperCollins Children's Books is a division of HarperCollins Publishers Ltd.

Text copyright © Ian Whybrow 2007
Illustrations copyright © Paul Howard 2007

The author and illustrator assert the moral right to be identified as the author and illustrator of the work.

A CIP catalogue record for this title is available from the British Library.

Visit our website at: www.harpercollinschildrensbooks.co.uk

Printed in Malaysia

The Magic Shoebox Farm

WRITTEN BY

IAN WHYBROW

ILLUSTRATED BY

PAUL HOWARD

HarperCollins *Children's Books*

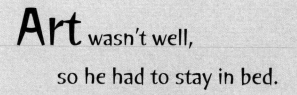**Art** wasn't well,

so he had to stay in bed.

"Telly?" suggested Dad.
But Art didn't feel like telly.

"Jelly-on-a-plate?"
said his little brother.
But Art didn't feel like jelly.

"I just want to **DO** something," said Art.

"I know," said Dad, "when I was little, Grandad made me a magic shoebox farm. I'll find it for you!"

"I bet it isn't magic," grumbled Art. "I bet it's just silly and old."

But you couldn't stop Dad. He left the shoebox on the bed anyway.

Art took no notice. But then the lid of the shoebox lifted up...

...all by itself.

Out climbed a funny red horse.

"Way-hey!

I'm Hoofer!" he said. "I'm from The Magic Shoebox Farm. I'm looking for the Mender. Oh dear, you aren't the Mender, are you? No. Sorry. Goodbye."

"W-W-Wait!" said Art. "What needs mending?"

"Red," said Hoofer. "He's our tractor. He's fallen over. Never mind. I'm sure *somebody* will help. Goodbye."

"Wait! I can mend things, I've got a toolbox," said Art, "*I'll* be the Mender."

"**Way-hey!**" said Hoofer. "I'd better ask Violet!"
He reached into the shoebox and pulled out
a purple piano and a violet cat.

"Hello, Violet," said Hoofer. "This is Art.
Can he be the Mender?"

"**Wee-wow!**" said Violet. "Of course.
But he'll need shrinking."
Violet played a little tune and sang…

Dinky donky

dunky dish

You can shrinky

if you wish

"Now you sing it," she said.

Violet played the dinky donky tune again and Art sang…

Dinky donky donky binky bish I can shrinky if I wish

Suddenly Art began to spin.

And he went smaller

and smaller

and smaller

until he was no bigger than

Violet's piano.

"Way-hey!

This way!" said Hoofer.

Art climbed into the shoebox
and suddenly he found himself
in a farmyard.

There they found Peewee the pig, making a mud aeroplane.
"This is Art, our new Mender," said Hoofer. "Red's in trouble
and he needs help."

"Unk unk"

said Peewee. "I can mend anything
with mud. I'll help you mend Red."

Up rushed Ma Sheep with
One and Two, her two tiny lambs.
"We can count, so we can help
mend Red. This way everyone."

So
Art
and **Hoofer**
and **Peewee**
and **Ma Sheep**
and **One**
and **Two**
all ran out of the meadow…

...and down to Bottom Field.
There they found
Red, lying on his
side, crying.
"I was just doing
a nice

Brrmmm

and my wheel fell off,"
he sobbed.

"I'll help mend you!"
said Hoofer.

Violet played the piano

and Hoofer did a
dance.

But that didn't help, not really.

"Counting will help!" said Maa.
And Maa and her lambs counted Red's
headlights. They went,

"Waa, Taa, Flea, Five, six!"

But that didn't help one bit.
Poor Red. He started to cry.
"I shall never

Brrmm

again!" he sobbed.

"That's **enough**
all of you! *I'm* the
Mender" shouted Art.

Art opened up his toolkit
and took out his tools.
"Come along, everyone,
lift Red up," said Art.

Then, when all the animals pulled and pushed,

Art gave a

dink

and a

donk

and a **HEAVE**

and a

honk

and a **screw** and a

SCRONK!

And on went Red's wheel,

nice and tight.

"He's done it!"

shouted the animals.

"Flea cheers for Mister Mender!"

said One and Two.

"Thank you, Mister Mender!" said Red. "All aboard!"

Art hopped on the seat.

"Look out! Here I come!" he said.

And off they went brrm_m brrm_{ming.}

They **brrm**med all over the Magic Shoebox Farm until it got late.

Brrmmmmm m . . .

Suddenly
they heard footsteps,
big ones.
"It's Dad!" said Art.
"Quick, Violet, play that
dinky donky tune!"
So Violet played the piano
and Art sang…

Dinky donky dunky dig

close my eyes and

I'll get BIG

Dad came in to Art's room.

"What a mess," he said, "I can see you're on the mend."

"That's because I'm the Mender!" said Art.

"Oh, really!" said Dad. "And what do you think of my shoebox farm?"

"Magic!"

said Art.